I ♥ LOVE MY TEACHER!

TODD PARR

Megan Tingley Books

LITTLE, BROWN AND COMPANY
NEW YORK BOSTON

This book was inspired by my love of teachers,
both those who encouraged me when I struggled in school
and those who support my books today.
Here's to all the great teachers in the world!

Love, Todd

Cover illustration copyright © 2016 by Todd Parr. Cover design by Saho Fujii and Lynn El-Roeiy.
Cover copyright © 2022 by Hachette Book Group, Inc.

Little, Brown and Company
Hachette Book Group
1290 Avenue of the Americas, New York, NY 10104
Visit us at LBYR.com

Originally published in hardcover by Little, Brown and Company in April 2016 as *Teachers Rock!*
First Trade Paperback Edition: May 2022

Little, Brown and Company is a division of Hachette Book Group, Inc.
The Little, Brown name and logo are trademarks of Hachette Book Group, Inc.

The publisher is not responsible for websites (or their content) that are not owned by the publisher.

Library of Congress Control Number: 2021944437

ISBN 978-0-316-54126-8

PRINTED IN CHINA

APS

10 9 8 7 6 5 4 3 2 1

They love coming to school, and

they make you love it, too!

Teachers help you learn

new things.

Teachers encourage you to be creative.

They help you find new talents.

Teachers read to you.

They play games with you, too.

Teachers are always willing to

help students in need.

Sometimes teachers make you laugh.

Sometimes they make you feel better.

Teachers let you share

all your favorite things.

Teachers make the classroom a great place to be.

They make sure students have everything they need.

make new friends.

of celebrations.

Teachers make you yummy snacks.

They take you on field trips.

Teachers love when your

families come to visit.

Teachers can be

just like you and me.

Teachers encourage you to try your best.

Most of all, they love to see you succeed.

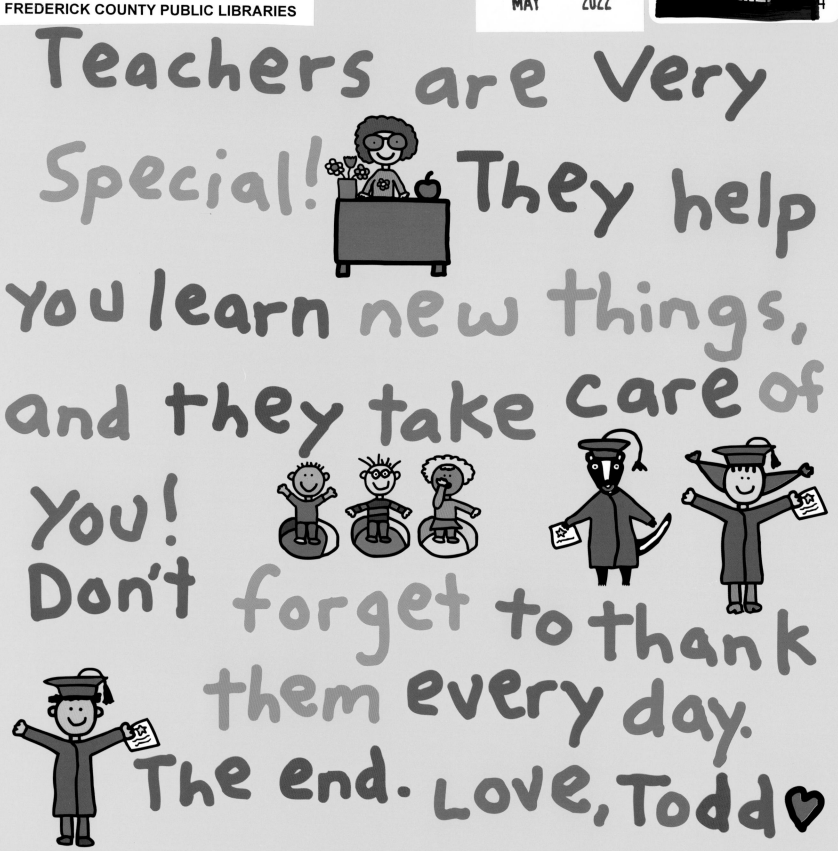

Teachers are Very Special! They help You learn new things, and they take care of You! Don't forget to thank them every day. The end. Love, Todd ♥